ST. LOUIS BLUES

SETH EDGARDE

BLACKBIRD BOOKS

NEW YORK • LOS ANGELES

A Blackbird Original, November 2014

Copyright © 2014 by Seth Edgarde

Manufactured in the United States of America.

The events and characters depicted in this book are fictional.

Cataloging-in-Publication Data

Edgarde, Seth.
St. Louis blues / Seth Edgarde.
p. cm.
1. St. Louis (Mo.)—Fiction. 2. Adultery—Fiction.
3. Traveling sales personnel—Fiction. I. Title.
PS3605.D4564 S25 2014 813'.54—dc22 2015930033

Blackbird Books
www.bbirdbooks.com
email us at editor@bbirdbooks.com

ISBN 978-1-61053-034-7

First Edition

10 9 8 7 6 5 4 3 2 1

ST. LOUIS BLUES

You walk out of a stiff rain into the side entrance of William McKinley High, Ames, Iowa, and, for a second, right back into eleventh grade. Only you're not eighteen anymore. You're a twenty-six year old woman in a business suit, carrying a briefcase, selling textbooks with a guy named Doug, a half step behind you.

You shake out your umbrella, feeling the drops hit your ankles. It's a quarter of two. Fifteen minutes before your next meeting, your next pitch.

"I'm going to the ladies' room," you tell him, twisting the fastener around your umbrella, still holding the briefcase, mildly annoyed that he isn't helping. You look back up, wondering which way to go, and there it is, right in front of you. You turn back and paste on a fake smile at Doug. "I'll be right back."

He looks at his watch. "Take your time."

You push the door open and enter even further into eleventh grade.

Three girls by the sink, huddled, talking, hushed. They see you. Silence. *Don't worry, I'm not a teacher* you think, glancing over at them, brief and sideways, but it doesn't matter.

Another girl, off in a corner smoking, tight jeans and makeup gives you a sloe-eyed look, the adult in a business suit. She's a little older, a senior maybe. She seems to realize that you're not faculty and too young to be a parent and goes back to her smoke, blowing out a huge fuck you plume, one arm tucked under the other.

You disappear into the first stall, but you can still hear the younger girls' whispers. They're probably talking about you, wondering who you are. Or maybe they've moved on. You decide you don't care.

You pull your briefcase up onto your lap and open it just as your phone rings. Duane. He's the last person you want to talk to right now—you won't in here anyway—so you push the button and send him to voicemail. You're still pissed at him from this morning. He should do his own damn shopping. And make his own damn breakfast.

You eye the black marker inside your briefcase and have the urge to add your own bit of graffiti to the stall wall: "Duane Bergin has a small dick." And then sign it, Kerry Bergin. Or better yet, *Mrs.* Duane Bergin. It's not true, but he deserves it. Imagining it there in black ink in a small clear patch next to the toilet paper dispenser, you grin to yourself. You know you won't do it, but it's still fun to think about.

Staring at the wall, you read some the other contributions: "Brittany Stadler stuffs her bra, Mr. Vogelman is hot, McKinley sucks!"

The whispering has stopped, and you hear the girls leave, but the cigarette smoke wafts over the door and settles on you. You don't really mind. Both your parents smoke, and it reminds you of the clubs where Duane plays when he can get a gig. Then you get annoyed all over again.

You pull a business card out of the front pouch: *Kerry Bergin, Sales Associate, Grantham Book Company, St. Louis, Missouri.* Slipping it in your side pocket, you feel how cheap it is as you close up your briefcase and exit the stall. Still wearing your still-wet raincoat, you wash your hands and try to dry your hair but to minimal effect. You shake out your coat and hope your shoes aren't ruined.

Doug looks up at you when come back out into the hall. "We still have a few minutes. Let's head over and practice our pitch."

All business, but that suits you fine. This is your first big account, and you're a little nervous. Duane didn't seem to notice that either.

Heading down the hallway, a pair of suits in a sea of jeans and pimples, you try to keep focus. Science textbooks, that's what you're selling. *If these kids only knew, we'd probably be assassinated.*

Following the numbers, your mind wanders, until Doug's voice breaks the spell. "Ladies first," he says, a little wry, like he's sending you in to be eaten by the faculty lions.

You open the door expecting the faculty lounge, but it's the auditorium.

"Are we in the right place?"

"Yeah, 307."

Looking down towards the stage, you see about a dozen people, adults, sitting, standing, and talking. You head down the aisle, Doug on your flank.

An older man sees him and extends his hand just as Doug hands him a card. "Doug Smith."

They shake hands. "Marty Vogelman."

You look at the grey old schoolmaster and have to suppress a laugh.

"I hope we're not late."

"No, not at all. Your timing's perfect. We had a meeting here before this one. Just broke up." He looks around. "Sorry for the oversized space. There's a flood in the faculty lounge. Happens every time we get a bad rain." He makes a sour face that seems to say "I told you so" to someone who's not there to be stung by the barb. "I'd say we picked the wrong contractor."

Vogelman's eyes move over to you, just behind Doug's rear quarter, and they light up when they meet yours.

"Kerry Bergin." You smile at him.

He smiles back with genuine pleasure and squeezes your hand, not in a creepy way but in the old-school way of a gentleman, and you suddenly understand why old man

Grantham likes to send at least one woman on each team. "Pleased to meet you, Miss Bergin."

You return his smile and don't correct him.

You meet everyone else in a flurry of names, none of which you remember as the butterflies take over in your stomach, and you stand at the foot of the stage and give your presentation, with Doug, the senior partner, looking on. You work on salary, but the company's margins are thin, and if you screw up and lose the sale, the old man'll find out about it before you get out of the parking lot.

So you hit all your points, putting it out of your mind that you yourself were a C+ student in high school, that you hated science and were terrible at it, that you never went to college, even though you lied on your resume and said you graduated from the University of Massachusetts at Lowell, because you thought it sounded impressive but not too much so, and thank god they never checked.

Heading into the home stretch, you blank out on one last set of statistics, but Doug pipes in seamlessly, and no one notices. You give out sample books, even though you don't have enough for everyone, and before you know it, you're in the parking lot.

"We might still lose the sale," Doug says, clicking open the doors to the white rental Ford compact.

Crestfallen, you look across the roof of the car at him but say nothing.

"Hey, relax," he says, not quite smiling. You both get into the car, and he starts it, looking over his left shoulder, backing out of the spot, even though you're upset and looking right at him. He seems to sense it and stops the car half out of the spot and looks right back at you. "Don't worry, you did great. If it doesn't happen, it's not because of you."

The relief and appreciation wash over you. "Thanks, Duane," you tell him.

You both pause for an awkward second. *Did you just call him Duane?*

"Doug," he corrects you, grinning.

Yes, you did. You feel your mouth hanging open, but no words are coming out.

He grins even wider at you, taking the car back the rest of the way out of the spot before shifting into drive and pulling out of the lot. "As long as you don't call *him* Doug," he says finally.

"Huh?"

"You know, call your husband by *my* name."

Oh god. Is *that* what he thinks? It's just because you've been replaying that argument from this morning in your head all day. You decide to shoot back. "I don't even *remember* your name," you tell him slyly. "What is it again? Marty Vogelman?"

He laughs. "I'm glad you've got a sense of humor."

This is only your second time out on the road and your first time with Doug. The month before last, it was a grizzled old saleswoman named Jillian—a real bitch and no help at all. Then she up and quit and so did Glyn, the new girl, leaving Grantham shorthanded and cementing your new job as the junior road girl. It also got you Doug as a sales partner.

He's a few years older than you—maybe 29 or 30—and you're pretty sure he's a native of St. Louis. He mentioned that he went to St. Louis University, anyway. He seems to know what he's doing, and you hope you learn enough fast enough to become a decent saleswoman. It's not what you pictured doing with your life, but it beats working at Starbucks in Saginaw, Michigan, which is where you're from and where you were when you met Duane, and you really need the money. God knows Duane isn't bringing it in.

"You still worried about that sale?"

"Oh. No, not really."

"Good." He keeps his eyes on the road and reaches into his pocket for a pack of cigarettes. "Mind if I smoke?" he asks, glancing over at you, a little guilty.

"No, go ahead," you tell him. Funny that he didn't think to offer you one.

His eyes dart to the dashboard. "What do you say we grab a drink before dinner?"

Oh, you get it, he was looking at the clock. It's not even 3:30, but you're done for the day, and it *has* been a long day, starting with that breakfast fight with Duane in your apartment in St. Louis at 6:30, through the flight to Iowa City, three pitch meetings—the last one yours—and hopefully at least one sale. And back to St. Louis in the morning. A quick drink sounds perfect. A quick drink, a nice dinner, and a good night's sleep. Early to bed and all that. You feel your phone buzz again, and you know it's Duane, but you're still too pissed to answer.

"What's a cigarette without a drink?" you ask.

"Exactly," he says, not getting the hint but looking a little befuddled.

Men are so stupid sometimes!

"No, seriously, a drink sounds great," you tell him to remove any doubt.

So you end up at a bar in downtown Ames, him with a whisky neat and you with a vodka sour. He tells you that he majored in business at SLU but ended up selling textbooks when the company he was working for went bankrupt. He's got a wife and two girls and seems happy, but you don't think he really is. You notice he isn't wearing a wedding ring. He orders another round and lights up another cigarette.

Halfway through your second drink, you're about to ask him what it means when a man criticizes everything you do for him, even though you're the one bringing home most of the money and even though you left your family in Michigan, married him, and moved to St. Louis so he could follow his dream to become a blues musician. But then his phone rings, and, unlike you, he takes it.

He steps away, phone to his ear, just as you catch sweet words coming from his mouth. You quickly realize they're for his daughter, and it makes your heart melt. He's back a few minutes later, and the moment's gone.

"Let's get out of here and get some food," he says, pulling his suit jacket on, then his trench coat over that. *You're the boss*, you think, resenting him a little for not consulting you, for not offering you that cigarette, for not giving you a chance to vent a little—about the job, Duane, anything— then you realize, he just had a fight with *his* wife.

You head to Denny's—not your first choice, but they've got some kind of discount for Grantham employees. He's quiet on the way over. Yeah, a fight. You order the meatloaf, and it sucks. He gets a roast beef sandwich that you're sure also sucks, but he doesn't seem to notice. You tell him that you're the third of four children, the second girl, that your sister is beautiful and brilliant, but you don't get along with her. You tell him about Duane but never work up the courage to ask for advice.

By the time you get to the hotel, you're ready for bed. It's only 8:30, but it'll be at least an hour and a half before you're asleep. You need to check in, get settled, wash up. And you know you have to talk to Duane. He didn't leave a message. Never does. But you can't go to sleep without calling him back, saying goodnight, telling him you love him. You do still love him, don't you?

You get out of the car and pull your overnight bag out of the back. Looking up, you see that it's an inexpensive motel, not cheap, and obviously clean and well cared for. Doug leads the way in. It's stopped raining now, and there's a certain fresh smell in the air that reminds you of home. You can't wait to be asleep in a warm bed.

The man behind the desk is Indian, older, with a white moustache that, contrasted with his dark skin, reminds you of a snow-capped mountain.

"Reservation for Smith," Doug says, back to business mode.

"Mr. and Mrs. Smith?" the man asks, smiling just a little.

You can tell Doug is annoyed. Probably gets this sort of thing all the time.

"No, *two* rooms. Both under my name—Doug Smith."

The man's smile fades, he puts on his glasses, and looks through the reservation book. It seems to take him forever, and Doug's getting antsy, shifting his weight from one foot to the other. He isn't the only one.

"Yes, reservation for Smith." He furls his eyebrows, flips the page over and back, and continues without looking up. "But it's for just one room."

"Well, we need two," Doug tells him, now really annoyed.

The man finally looks up and wobbles his head the way Indians do to indicate *no*. "I'm sorry, I just have the one room," the man tells him, apologetic and now almost grimacing. "Football weekend."

Well, ok, you think, we'll go somewhere else. Let the senior partner work it out.

Doug nods, understanding something that you don't, and you wait for someone to say something, until the Indian man wobbles his head again and finishes the debate off for good. "You won't find another room tonight for fifty miles," he says bluntly. Then he gives Doug his most apologetic look yet. "Oklahoma State."

"Huh?" you say, more baffled than annoyed.

The men grin at each other, and Doug looks back at you. "Oklahoma State *University*. They're playing Iowa State here in Ames on Saturday. Place is probably booked solid." He turns back to the man behind the desk for verification. Men love to be right.

The Indian man smiles and wobbles his head *yes* this time. "Maybe we'll win this year."

Doug gives him a sideways glance as if to say *I don't think so*.

With more than a little worry, you try to catch his eye to find out what the plan is, but you can see he doesn't know, he's thinking, trying to figure it out. Men love to do that too.

Finally, he looks back at the man. "Does that room have twin beds?"

Twin beds? Are you kidding? Is that the best you can come up with? You're on the brink of telling him that you're not staying in the same room with him even if he has to sleep in the car, when the Indian man starts to talk, grinning again but in an ironic way this time. "One bed, king size."

You open your mouth to speak up, before it's too late, but you can already see Doug shaking his head no.

"So, what? That's it? We're stuck?" you say to the snow-capped moustache.

"I can give you a cot," the man offers.

"Great, a cot," you say with all the sarcasm you can muster.

Doug looks at you, with the stoic air of a gentleman, almost chivalrous. "It's ok, Kerry, you take the room, I'll sleep in the car."

You look at him, puppy dog face, blue eyes, just as tired as yours, and you begin to buckle. "No, don't be ridiculous."

"Really, it's ok," he tells you, and you can see that he means it.

"No, Doug, it's ok, you're not sleeping in the car," you tell him, sounding like a wife. Then you make some half-witted remark about having two brothers, and, next thing you know, it's you, Doug, a king-size bed, and a cot in a second floor motel room with two carry-on suitcases and only one suitcase rack.

He lets you take the rack and even puts your suitcase on it for you, as you realize that you don't even have a t-shirt to sleep in.

You end up sleeping in your clothes, on top of the bed-spread, not even washing up properly. At least you get to brush your teeth.

He sleeps in his boxers, and it embarrasses you, but you glance away, trying not to show it, and he doesn't seem to notice.

You don't sleep well, stuffed in your business suit, but he keeps the air on all night, so the temperature ends up being just about right anyway.

When you wake up, you feel awful, still in your clothes, sweaty, the room air-conditioner clammy.

His bed is empty, and you get up to see where he is—the bathroom maybe—when you see his note: *Went to get break-fast. Didn't want to wake you.* That's nice, you think to yourself. Considerate. He probably knew that you wanted your privacy, and you run to take a shower while you have the chance, taking a change of clothes with you.

Hot water running over you, you wonder if he'll think to bring something back for you, even just coffee. It was the kind of thing Duane used to do when you were first married.

Duane. You forgot to call him last night before you went to bed. Your heart sinks, and you feel like crying. Your marriage is falling apart, and you have no idea what to do about it.

You finish your shower and squeeze into your jeans, checking yourself out in the mirror. You're not ugly but far from perfect—hips too big, face too ordinary. Certainly not as pretty as your sister. She's on the west coast, living with her boyfriend, working for a modeling agency. She even did some modeling herself for a while, showing up in a Victoria's Secret ad in Esquire Magazine. Yeah, she's always been the pretty one. And the oldest. And Jimmy was the baby. And Ted, the oldest boy. And then there's you. Kerry, the worker bee. Number two daughter. You even have to share being a middle child.

It's true, your dad was a little embarrassed when he saw Jeanette in a lace thong in a men's magazine, but still, you could tell he was proud of her: Proud of her sheer beauty, proud that she had made the big time. At any rate, now she was in management, making a ton of money, her college degree in hand. And you, you're selling textbooks to kids in Iowa, living in a one-bedroom with your black, wannabe blues musician husband, in the warehouse district of St. Louis, just trying to make ends meet.

You brush your hair out into a ponytail, fastening your hair tie as you leave the bathroom, and you see that Doug is there, just walked in, holding a small white bag. He did get you breakfast. You smile at him, and he glances you over, expressionless.

"We don't have any meetings," you say, protesting what you think is a look of disapproval at your jeans and blouse.

"No," he says, knitting his eyebrows. "Why?"

"Because you looked at me like I should be wearing something else," you say, noting with your eyes that *he's* wearing a suit. The same suit, in fact, that he wore yesterday.

He grins at you. "Relax," he says. "I just travel light." His grin turns to a smirk. "No meetings. Just a plane back to St. Louis. I promise."

You suddenly realize that your arms are crossed, and you're prone on one foot, hip sticking out in accusation, and you feel like a fool. *I'm such a bitch,* you think to yourself. *No wonder my marriage is falling apart.*

"I'm sorry," you tell him, unfolding your arms, and grounding yourself on both feet. Then you say it. "I had a huge fight with my husband, and I'm just a little wound up."

His smile fades a little as he puts the bag down on the dresser. "Occupational hazard," he says. "My wife doesn't like me out on the road so much either." Then he looks away, almost embarrassed. "Especially not with a pretty girl."

There's an awkward pause, and you get it now. It's the first time he's seen you in jeans, *tight jeans*, and he liked what he saw, and now he's said too much, and he's embarrassed.

"Anyway," he breaks the silence. "I got you a little breakfast."

"Thanks, Doug," you say, with a tender smile.

"It's just a cup of coffee and a donut." He looks up at you, and you notice his clear, brilliant, blue eyes, sharpening his oval face and perfect white teeth, all under a neat crop of tight dark curls. "I hope you like jelly."

"It's perfect," you tell him, even though you hate jelly donuts.

You drink the coffee, black, thinking of that line about how you like your coffee like your men: strong and black, and you tell Doug, and you both laugh about it. And you mention how Duane's not that strong and pretty light-skinned for a black guy. "The sensitive artist type," you say, and the joke dies. But Doug's on to the next thing, eyeing that jelly donut, and you offer it to him, telling him that you have to watch your figure, even though that's not the reason. You can't tell whether he's buying it or not, but he's half done while you're still thinking about it.

When you get to the car, he piles the bags in the trunk, and you both get in, but he doesn't start the car right away, looking at you for a second before speaking.

"You know, we saved seventy bucks on a second room last night." He looks at you with those blue eyes again. A little mischievous. "They give us the budget ahead of time, and they never check receipts."

You don't quite get it.

"It would be a real pain to have to give the company back the cash for the extra room last night and have them re-do all that accounting." He pulls out some money. "It was over eighty bucks with tax." He hands it to you.

You take it hesitantly and look down at two twenties in your hand. You look up at him. "What's this?"

"Your share," he says.

That's stealing, you think, but you just look into those baby blues, shake your head gently, and hand the money back to him, your fingers touching briefly in the interchange. "I can't," you tell him. But the truth is that you could really use the cash. Duane brings in practically nothing, and you only make $35,000 a year.

He takes the bills and puts them back in his pocket. "I'll hold it for you if you change your mind," he says, starting the car, and heading out.

You feel like you've just stuck your finger into an electric socket. *Stealing from the company. God, he's such a bad boy.*

Then he makes it worse. "You know, we'll be on the road at least a few days a month," he says. "From now on." He pauses, as if to let that sink in. "And some of the hotels in the big cities, like Cincinnati or Cleveland, are a lot more than eighty bucks a night with tax."

You get it now. Totally. Out on the road together once a month, usually for the better part of a week. Tell the company you're taking two hotel rooms but only take one and pocket the money for the other, even split, 50-50, you and Doug. "I figure it'd be about two grand a year apiece," he tells you. And the whole thing begins to scare you, like that charge going through you, and you're not sure what you feel.

"I can't," you tell him again, and he seems to sense your fear, backing off.

Then his cell phone rings. He answers. Old man Grantham. Doug puts him on speaker phone, and your heart races.

"You and Kerry," he says. "I'd like to see you in my office when you get back."

"Sure thing, Mr. Grantham," Doug says, the ever-confident golden-haired boy. "First thing Monday morning."

"No. Today," the old man says. "Come from the airport. I want to see you as soon as you get back."

Your blood runs cold. It's like he knows what you were talking about. Even though that's impossible. But still, it can't be good. In to see the boss straight off the plane. And you're in jeans.

Doug hangs up, and you look at him. "I need to change."

He looks over, eyes darting down to your jeans. "Don't worry, he knows we're traveling."

He reaches inside his jacket but comes up empty. Looking for a cigarette. Then you realize: It's about the account. The pitch yesterday. The verdict is in, and the old man wants to see the two of you. And Doug wants a cigarette, because he's nervous.

You drive the rest of the way to the airport in silence, only stopping to talk about which way to your gate once you've returned the rental car, until you're both seated waiting for the plane.

"Don't worry, I think we got the sale. And it's *my* butt if we didn't."

You can see he's relaxed a little but still fidgeting for that cigarette. You could use one yourself.

"I've been there for four years, and I haven't seen him fire a pretty girl yet."

This guy *is* a bad boy. Stealing from the company, flirting with a married woman. A married woman who he knows just had a fight with her husband. You cross your arms and look over at him, but he's already checking his email and ignoring you, if he's noticing you at all.

You have to admit, you like bad boys. They're fun and exciting. You used to think Duane was one, but it turns out he's just another lump. You slump in your seat feeling like a slob again, and wanting to go to the ladies' room to change back into your suit. But the plane starts boarding, and there's no time.

It's a short flight to St. Louis, but you manage a couple of Bloody Marys, finally loosening up, and telling Doug about your life. You can't for the life of you figure out why, besides a couple of shots of vodka, you're telling him anything personal about yourself, but those baby blues melt you, and you end up prattling on.

He actually gives good advice. He tells you to cut the guy a break. He's probably having a rough time of it. Not making any money, not getting anywhere with his music, and you realize he's right. But you still lay into him anyway.

"The guy drags me off to St. Louis 'to play the blues,'" you say, in mock quotes with your fingers. "He's a sax player, and St. Louis is famous for its piano blues." You brush back your hair in frustration. "No wonder the jerk can't get a gig."

Doug nods but still sticks up for the guy. "Maybe he thought that'd make him stand out."

Now you nod. "Yeah. That's what he says. Maybe he's right." You exhale, regretting how much you've said and turn to ask him about his wife, but the pilot comes over the intercom to announce that you're landing, and the opportunity is gone, the tension of the meeting with the boss kicking in.

"What's he like?" you ask on the way out of the plane.

"Grantham?" Doug says. "Haven't you met him?"

"No. I've only been with the company four months. I was hired by Barbara in personnel. I've only seen Mr. Grantham in the hallway a couple of times, and he didn't seem to notice me."

Doug nods and flashes a knowing look. "Believe me, he knows who you are. He knows everything that goes on in that company. At least personnel-wise." You're in the airport now, the two of you, rushing through with your carry-ons on wheels, him in his day-old suit, still not too badly rumpled, and you in your tight jeans. "You got to understand, textbooks, it's a people business, so he knows all the people and makes sure he's got the right folks in the right place. He's a hand-shaker, a back-slapper. He knows everyone. The president of SLU. The governor." He turns to you with a knowing smile. "The nuts and bolts, the accounting and all that stuff, he leaves to the underlings. But the people he's got representing his company, his name, he knows every one of us."

You make it to the curb out front, and Doug grabs a cab. He tells you more about the company and preps you for the meeting on the way over. "Just smile and be yourself. You did great yesterday. There's nothing to worry about."

When you enter the building, it feels strange to be at the office in jeans, but it's after five, and almost everyone is gone. Oddly, entering the boss's office with a suitcase, for a meeting late on a Friday afternoon, makes you feel important, and you try to stretch that into confidence.

You enter the executive suite, and the secretary smiles at Doug. She's in her fifties, but he's probably been flirting with her since the day he showed up. You see her name plate: *Jenny Garth*, and you feel like laughing. She's middle-aged, short and mousy, with dark hair—nothing like the actress—but you realize that she probably had the name first.

"He's on the phone," she says. Then, quickly, as you start to sit, "Oh, no, he's off now. You can go in."

From a split second easing back to full tension, you go upright again, and Doug leads the way, suitcases in tow.

"Doug, Kerry," he says, smiling and getting halfway up. "Sit down." *He's smiling. Good sign.* His sits back down and plants his elbows on the desk then puts his hands together. He's old, and his knuckles are knobby with liver spots. It reminds you of your grandfather.

"Sorry to drag you in on a Friday afternoon, fresh off a plane, but I had to tell you in person. We got the contract with McKinley." Then he looks right at you. "Apparently Dr. Vogelman was quite taken with you, *Miss* Bergin."

You're too shocked to even smile back for a second, until it hits you: You got the contract. Your pitch, your first pitch, got the sale. And you break into a smile.

But the old man looks at both of you, eyes sparkling, leaning forward even further, until you can practically touch him, and you realize there's more. "And he's on the school board. He's going to recommend us to every other school in the district."

The truth is, you don't really know too much about the textbook business, but you know *this* has to be good.

The old man finally leans back, done with his news, folding his hands contentedly against his breastbone, almost like old King Louis himself, and you look over at Doug from the corner of your eye, and he really is the golden-haired boy, even with the dark curls. And you smile at each other, the awkward moment in the car now gone, or at least in the background.

"You two make quite a team," the old man says, looking you over.

"It was all Kerry," Doug tells him, laying it on a little, but you don't mind.

Five minutes later, you're heading out of the building, relieved and wound-up at the same time. And dreading going home to face Duane.

So you end up going for a drink with Doug. You're not that anxious to get back home, and you need to unwind. Another Bloody Mary does the trick. Then a second.

You talk about St. Louis, the saxophone, and the blues. Doug tells you all about the great sax players, a couple even from right there in St. Louis, the jump blues piano town. He mentions King Curtis, Roosevelt Sykes, and Dave Sanborn.

"King Curtis was from Texas, Roosevelt Sykes played the piano—" you start.

"Yeah, I know, and Sanborn's a white guy."

You laugh in the middle of a swig of beer and almost lose it. "He's actually Duane's favorite." You wipe your mouth.

"Hey, I like Sanborn." He takes a swig himself. "Of course, I'm allowed."

"What, 'cause *you're* a white guy?"

He looks straight ahead, taking another long gulp. "'Cause we're both actually *from* St. Louis."

You laugh again, even though it wasn't that funny. But you're feeling good and, you realize, a bit woozy.

"I should get home," you tell him.

But five minutes later, you're still talking.

He tells you the old man is probably going to send the two of you out on the road even more, to some of the bigger cities, and you find yourself kind of looking forward to it. He doesn't mention it, and neither do you, but you know that he's thinking it: more money to steal.

"Now's the time to ask for a raise," you say.

Now he laughs, until he sees you're serious. "Good luck with that."

"What, you don't think we've earned it?"

"No, you're right, this means a ton of money to the company."

"So?"

"You'll never see a cent of it. The old man's as tight as a rusty bolt." He looks at you. "What are you making? 45?"

"Your face falls and gives you away."

"40?"

He shakes his head. "Whatever you're making, you'll be lucky to get a five percent raise at your one-year review." He takes another swig and lights up a cigarette from the pack he bought on the way in. This time you take one without asking and he lights you both without missing a beat. "Including the cost of living increase."

You're not sure whether to believe him or not, but you do. You decide to put in for a raise anyway, first thing Monday morning.

Then he changes the subject, telling you to lighten up on Duane, and you decide he's right. It all makes you kind of horny—booze and blues, hotel rooms and ripping off the company, and that winning pitch and closing the deal, and all of the sudden, you want to rush home, make a great dinner, and make love to your sweet, sax-playing husband.

But you don't even have enough money in your purse to buy groceries, putting those two twenties Doug offered you out of your mind, and you decide you don't need the food, just Duane.

"I've got to go," you say, trying again.

And he nods, putting out his cigarette, half-smoked but still enough to have done the trick.

You hang on to yours, finishing off your beer between puffs, and you look at him and pause for a second like you're going to hug him, because it kind of feels right, but he's just a co-worker, and it's just another Friday after work, so you leave with a "See you Monday" and a moment later, you're out on the street.

And you hear blues coming from the club another moment later. Looking at your watch, you realize it's eight, and there's a local band coming on, and you kind of wish they had come on earlier, but it makes you even hornier or maybe it's just the nicotine rush.

You go to hail a cab, but you don't want to waste the money and you're not even sure you have enough, so you decide to walk.

It's only about ten blocks, but it feels longer, and you wonder if Duane is home and how pissed off he'll be, until finally, you're at the front of your place, and you let yourself in and climb up the stairs.

It's an old warehouse, converted, dark and industrial, but it's home and you like it. When you get to your apartment, you let yourself in, and it's dark. You realize he's not home yet, but you call his name anyway, and there's no answer, so you turn on the lights.

Your sweater is still sprawled across the couch where you left it the morning before in the hustle to get to the airport. So are the unpaid bills on the crate you use as a living room table.

The apartment is just a big room on the upper floor of the old warehouse. Loft-like, the ceiling is at least twenty-five feet high with ducts running up under the roof. The walls to the kitchen only go up about eight feet, having been added later, at the time of conversion, and only covering two sides. The third side is the brick wall of the exterior, and the fourth is open. The kitchen is small, which you always found odd, because there's plenty of space to have made it bigger.

There really is no bedroom, a futon on the opposite wall, next to another smaller crate that serves as a nightstand and a large armoire on the other side. There are two dressers, one from IKEA, and one looking like some kind of antique left by Lewis and Clark next to it.

Only the bathroom is fully enclosed, having been left-over from the original, the toilet and sink—a twin-spigot model—about as ancient as you've ever seen. And even the shower-tub, which was probably added later but still well before the more recent conversion, is at least fifty years old.

There are a couple of windows on the far side and two more on the adjacent wall, but they face north and riverside, so the apartment is generally dark, especially after noon and especially in the winter.

Duane put up a neon sign on the alley-side wall, and he even managed to get a broken Coke machine to decorate the space opposite the bathroom. All-in-all, it's kind of a funky apartment, but hardly luxurious. And it's not in the best neighborhood. But it is big, and it's cheap.

You check your phone and see that it's almost twenty-five after eight. You're not sure when Duane's coming home, but you decide to dim the lights and get naked. You put on "Slow Walk" by Sil Austin, stripping to his slow, sultry, tenor sax, until it's just you, four walls, and an empty futon.

Still naked, you do a little dance, sexy, and easy over to the bed, stopping at the foot and sitting then lying back and stretching to the head, arching your pelvis into the air, ready, thinking to yourself how perfect it would be for him to enter right then and half-expecting him to do so, but he doesn't, and you lie back and wait. On top of the sheets, still naked, at first. Then under the sheets. Then you fall asleep. And when you wake up, it's three a.m., and he's still not home. And you go back to sleep until seven and get up and pace, furious. You call him, and he doesn't answer, and you get worried and think to call the police or one of his friends, but you barely know any of them.

By the time ten rolls around, you're in sweats, no under-wear, somehow thinking that that's still important, and you decide to have breakfast, pouring a bowl of cereal, Count Chocula, which you hate, but you bought because he likes it, when he walks in.

"Where the fuck have you been?"

He glances at you for a second, and you notice he was smiling, but that's gone now. "Out," he says. Striding past you and your Count Chocula and over to the bed where takes his shirt and pants off.

"You don't call?" you say, the nasty wife, but you're too mad to bother to stop.

And he looks at you, harsh and angry, and you get it. You didn't call him, so you've got no right, and even though it's different, it isn't really, at least not to him, and maybe he's right, but you're too mad to let him be, and just like that, it's turned mean and petty.

"Look, I'm tired," he says, already in bed, and you wish he'd been there a few hours ago. "Can we talk about this later?"

You want to tell him what he missed out on last night, but you've got a lump in your throat. You put on socks and sneakers and grab ten bucks, heading for the door, hoping he'll ask where you're going, so you can say "out," but he doesn't, sleeping or pretending to be by the time you exit.

You know he was probably out with his musician friends, at some club, talking about Albert King or Lonnie Johnson and maybe even jamming a little, but part of you wonders if he's having an affair, if he didn't miss out on anything last night after all. And you burst into tears halfway down the stairs, sitting to cry, listening to the empty warehouse echo before you finally compose yourself and head out for a cup of coffee and a walk along the river to clear your head.

You feel awful, no panties, no bra, loose sweats and your makeup probably smeared all over your face, but you wipe your eyes on your sleeve and walk the two blocks toward the river to the local coffee shop, a semi-cool, semi-yuppie place on Kosciusko called the St. Louis Brown after some old baseball team, and you hope the kid behind the counter doesn't notice you've been crying. Then you decide you don't care, thinking about Duane as you sip your black coffee, realizing you're going to need a bathroom as you make your way down to 1st Street then South Wharf, heading towards downtown and the Gateway Arch.

When you get to the park, you sit, cross-legged on the grass under the arch, looking up, still amazed, amazed that someone built it, that it's so solid but so delicate, so big and imposing up close.

You remember the first time you and Duane went up to the top, when you first got to St. Louis. You were terrified but exhilarated. And gratified to find out that the guy who designed it was Finnish, like your mom's family, and Duane teased you about it, but he never teases you about anything anymore.

You were only nineteen then, just married, in love, excited to be in the big city. And a little scared. So far from your family. That was almost seven years ago.

It's a nice day out. Late summer, still warm, and you watch the river traffic along the Mississippi until that coffee finally makes its way through you.

Heading back inland to downtown, you ditch into the Millennium Hotel to pee, embarrassed at the way you look but trying not to show it, leaving the attendant a buck before you go.

It's almost eleven now, but you don't feel like going home yet, and you still have six dollars in your pocket. There's an old theatre that shows silent movies, just inside Soulard, west of 7th, that charges three bucks for all day and three more for a bucket of popcorn and a soda on Saturdays before noon.

Twenty minutes later, you buy a ticket from the old woman who runs the place and plant your butt dead-center, ten rows back. There's no one else in the theatre, and you wonder how they stay in business, but slowly, more people come in—an old guy in back, a couple of kids, and some people in the balcony.

You watch for a couple of hours—Harold Lloyd, Buster Keaton, and then Charlie Chaplin in *The Gold Rush,* which you've seen before. And then a movie called *The Crowd* that shows New York in 1928, and you can't believe how dense that city is, and even though you've never been there, it makes you glad you live in St. Louis.

It's almost three before you wander back home, and Duane's not there. Not even a note. You take a shower, put on shorts and a t-shirt, and call your mother.

"Everything's good, mom. I made a big sale this week," you tell her.

She tells you how terrific that is, and you don't let on that anything else is wrong, because you don't want to worry her, and you're tired.

You hang up and are about to call Duane when he comes in.

"Are you going out tonight?" you ask him. You don't say whether that means him alone or the two of you, but you're hoping.

"No, I'm beat."

You nod. You think to tell him that you could change into something sexy, but you're still kind of mad and don't want to give in. And the fear that he'll reject you takes over, and before you can say anything more, he asks you to order Chinese for delivery, and you're relieved that he's staying in and glad because you can put it on your card because your bank account is empty and you don't have any cash.

You sit and hardly talk, eating then watching a kung fu movie on TV. He probably thinks you hate it, but the guys are really ripped, and you love watching them move.

You sleep in on Sunday and watch him read the Post-Dispatch before you go to do laundry at a place on the other side of downtown. It should make you mad, but you're glad to get out of the house and have something to do.

And then, before you know it, it's Monday again.

You're feeling good, good about work, the sale, that the boss likes you, and you put on a red dress that you've been saving even though it's kind of hot with a slip and hose. And Duane notices but in a kind of accusative way.

"What are you all dressed up for?"

You haven't told him about the sale, because you don't want to make him feel bad, but since he asked . . . "I had my first big sale on Friday," you tell him, making brief eye contact with him in the mirror as you put on lipstick.

"That's great," he says, half-convincingly, probably hoping that means more money but maybe resenting you for bringing it in.

You shrug and turn to face him, giving him a smile, but he's got his head down and doesn't see.

A minute later, you're out the door and on the bus to work.

You spend half the day filling out paperwork, wondering what you're doing in such nice clothes, feeling less like the superstar saleswoman by the minute. Until Doug comes in and walks over to your cubicle.

"How's Grantham's number one saleswoman?" he asks.

You turn around, glad to abandon the paperwork for a second. "Getting paper cuts and blisters at the moment."

He looks at the forms. "Well you know, you make the sale, you got to do the paperwork."

The small talk is killing you. "As soon as I'm done with this, I'm going to put in for a raise."

He shakes his head. "You've been here four months."

"I know."

"Look, you got a lot going for you—"

"Yeah, I know, I'm pretty, but I haven't been here very long, I didn't go to college, and don't have much experience, at least selling textbooks."

He nods. "Yeah. That's about the size of it."

You look at him with slightly pleading eyes. He just walked in, and he's still holding his briefcase and coffee, and you know he wants to sit down and read his email or whatever before he starts the day, and you're keeping him here. But he's the only person you can talk to at the company, and you know he's interested, bad boy and all. "If I can just get the old man to see that I've put in for a raise . . ."

He shakes his head. "He'd be the first one to turn you down." He shrugs and starts in on his coffee. "Gotta pay your dues."

You don't want to argue with him, but you're sure he's wrong. The old man likes you. You brought in a whole damn school district in Iowa. Grantham's already a zillionaire and he's going to get even richer. What's another few bucks to the girl who helped make it happen?

Then you think about how little they're paying you now, and all those bills, and that lazy bum Duane. "They're paying me thirty-five a year. I can't pay the freaking rent."

He looks at you with surprise and empathy. *Been there, done that.* And you wonder how much he makes, but you don't dare ask.

He purses his lips a little, like he wants to tell you but says nothing, and you read between the lines. *I'm not making that much more than you, and I've been here four years with a wife and two kids. And I've got a degree.*

Taking another sip, he gestures to you. "Hey, what do I know? Maybe you'll get lucky. The old man *does* like you. Go for it."

But you know what he thinks, and you're determined to prove him wrong. Or maybe you're just desperate.

Two hours later, you glide into the old man's office on your red pumps, smiling at Jenny Garth as you stop at her desk.

"I don't have an appointment," you tell her. "But I just wanted to thank Mr. Grantham again for Friday." You put your hand to your chest, but before she can react, Grantham walks in, heading to his office with another man who you recognize from accounting, middle-aged, in a suit.

And you turn to grab his attention and bump into him and he grazes across your chest, and you both ignore the accident but you're hoping it'll play to your advantage as you plant on a huge smile.

"Mr. Grantham."

He looks a little shocked, distracted. And you wonder if he even remembers you.

"It's Kerry Bergin, sir."

And he looks at you like you're an idiot for thinking that he doesn't know who you are, and you continue, ignoring the misstep.

"I just wanted to thank you again for seeing us on Friday and telling us about the sale." You look right into his eyes. Blue and clear, and, you think, showing a hint of affection for the excited young sales associate. "You really made my weekend."

He smiles now, with the other man looking on, and looks down for a second, then at you, a little embarrassed but very pleased. "Oh, that's quite alright my dear. It was my pleasure."

The moment's over, and you're about to turn and leave, but the old man looks at the other man and gestures to him, looking at you. "This is Bob Beck, head of accounting."

Then at you, giving him a more prolonged look. "This is Kerry Bergin, our newest rising star in sales."

You're in, you think, turning on your heels a moment later, almost twirling that dress, feeling great and looking it, you hope. "Pretty girl," you hear one of them say, thinking you're out of earshot. *Yes, in. Definitely,* you think.

You file the paperwork with Emily in Human Resources who assures you it will cross Grantham's desk at some point. "Before the end of the week," she says when you ask again.

You want to ask what she thinks of your chances, but she's not particularly friendly or engaged, so you let it go.

One day slides into the next, and before you know it, it's Friday. It seems like you hardly see Duane anymore. In the morning and late at night when he comes back from wherever he's been. And that's about it. You don't even fight anymore. In fact, you hardly talk, like you're leading separate lives. He doesn't even know that you put in for a raise. And you don't even ask where he goes every night, coming back at two or three in the morning, long after all the clubs have closed.

You don't see any lipstick on him, and you don't smell any perfume, but there's no cigarette smoke either, a hallmark of the music scene. Wherever he's going, it's not there.

He's cheating. You're sure of it. You go into the ladies' room at work, lock yourself in the end stall by the beveled glass window there on the ninth floor, sit down still clothed, and cry quietly for a good twenty minutes.

You fix your makeup and head back to your desk. It's still only mid-morning, and you can't wait for lunch. You've been eating with Doug every day now, and it's a welcome break. He's told you all about his two little girls.

The younger one needs braces and the older one, who's just turned ten, wants an iPhone.

"Ten?" you had asked, incredulous. It seems impossible. But he tells you he's thirty-two—older than he looks. Certainly older than you thought.

You replay it in your mind, there at your desk, until your eye catches sight of an interoffice envelope next to your keyboard. Then an email from Eric, head of the sales force, then another one from Doug, and you pause for a second, trying to decide which to open first.

You undo the string and pull out two stapled pages from the manila envelope. It's your raise application, and you stare, heart racing, trying to make sense of it for a second. You flip it over, but there's nothing else. Just the application. Then you check the envelope and notice another white sheet still stuck inside. Pulling it out, you see a letter on company stationary. Official. One sheet, two lines. *Thank you for inquiring about the possibility of a salary increase . . .*

You skip through, catching a few words to the end. *Review . . . One year . . .*

We regret that we are unable to accommodate your request at this time. This is not a reflection of your performance to date.

Your heart sinks and your anger builds. *Not a reflection of your performance to date.* Glad to hear it! You look to the bottom, and there it is, the signature: Edmund G. Grantham, Jr., President.

You can hardly believe it. He screwed you. That broken-down old prick! After all that.

Then you think: The emails. Yeah, what's in those emails? You wonder what's next, and you open your inbox.

First Eric, then Doug. They're sending you to Cincinnati. All next week. With Doug. *Remember, as always, your representing the Grantham name. Always present it in the best possible light.*

Your not *you're.* The idiot can't even spell right. And *you* didn't even graduate from college. Yeah, present the company in the best light.

Two more mails come in, from Eric again then Doug, and it takes you a minute to catch up. They need you to go out on Sunday night—seven a.m. meeting on Monday morning—and you won't be back until Saturday. Meetings and pitches, all week. You look at the list. Must be every school district. At least it seems like it.

You see that Doug is angling for a better hotel—"Closer to the airport," he writes, like that makes a difference. And they give it to him! All you need's a pair of pants and a dick.

You call Doug, anxious to go out to lunch and vent, but he doesn't answer. Just as well. You'd probably end up venting at him. For being right. For being a man. For getting that hotel room by the airport.

It's not his fault, and at the moment, it seems like he's your only friend. You head out to lunch on your own, planning to take at least an hour when your cell rings. Personnel. Cathy this time. You let it go to voicemail, picking up the message a minute later: They need you to fill out paperwork for the trip. And take a urine test. A urine test!

You call Doug again. On his cell. He meets you outside.

"Come on, let's go for a dog. I know a place downtown."

You look at him like he's crazy, but then you realize, a *hot* dog. But he doesn't seem to understand your confusion and continues.

"It's less than five minutes away. Best Polish in the city."

"Huh?"

He shakes his head to swat the confusion aside and touches your shoulder gently to move you in the right direction. "Polish sausage," he tells you.

He's right about the hot dog, and by the time you've finished nursing the rest of your Diet Coke, he's talked you down from the ledge.

"I wasn't going to quit," you tell him.

"I know," he says.

You slurp the bottom, unladylike, and look up at him and laugh. "I'm a jerk."

"Why? Because you want a decent paycheck?"

You nod and laugh a little.

"Just fill out the forms and take the drug test. No big deal. I know a great rib place in Cincinnati. You like ribs?"

You look at him like he's the jerk this time. "We live in St. Louis."

"Hey, you're talking to a native here." Soft peddling his St. Louis bonafides again . . . "But I'm telling you, this is the best place I've ever been to. Including Chicago."

You look down at your empty cup. He's trying to cheer you up, and it's working. You certainly appreciate the effort. But you're still broke, and your marriage is falling apart, and now you have to go back to the office and pee into a cup in order to sell freaking textbooks to a bunch of kids who'll probably never read them anyway.

But you'll do it. Because you have to.

By the time you get home, it's almost seven. You're exhausted. You think about the week as you step inside you're place and pop off your shoes. You're not even expecting Duane to be home and he's not. But the bills are still there, where they've been all week.

You walk past them to your dresser and change into shorts and a t-shirt then head over to the fridge. Nothing but milk. And that Count Chocula. You notice the milk is past the expiration date, and you put it back. You spy a beer in the back. One of the local micro brews that Duane likes, and you take it, walking over to the couch, plopping down, and turning on the TV.

You zone out, watching Andy McCarthy in a Hallmark romance, finishing your beer in the first five minutes and wanting another one for the next hour and a half. You take a shower and go to bed.

You get up early the next day, putting on your shorts and t-shirt, careful not to wake Duane—you don't even remember him coming in—and head to the park and the grass under the arch.

You call your best friend, Stacy, back in Michigan, and you talk for almost three hours. You tell her everything, and you realize how much you miss her. And home. And you realize how lonely you are.

"You can always hop on a bus and come back here," she tells you.

"I know," you say, feeling her warmth wash over you. "But I can't."

You tell her about Doug, "this guy at the office," and she sounds excited for you. And you tell her about the money. Stealing. "Wow" is about all she can muster.

It's almost eleven by the time you're done, and you head over to the silent movie theater again, staying almost the whole day this time. You decide you like silent movies better than new ones, even though you know you'll change your mind at the next Hallmark flick.

You pick up a frozen pizza on the way home and pack for your trip to Cincinnati.

Duane comes back early and sees the suitcase. His face drops, and you realize he thinks you're leaving, leaving *him*. It's nice to see that he still cares.

You place a blouse in a corner. "I've got to go to Cincinnati tomorrow."

"Huh?"

You keep packing, keep talking without really looking at him. Red pumps in another corner. Black ones in next to them. Hose, slips, a pantsuit. "We're pitching to every school district in the city. I'll be gone all week." You debate for a second and then throw in the red dress.

"Oh," he says, standing there like a lump.

"I got a frozen pizza in the oven." You gesture over to the kitchen, looking right at him, not warm but not unfriendly either.

"Thanks."

You leave the suitcase on the bed, ready to share the pizza with him.

He goes to the fridge, and you know what's next.

"Where's my beer?"

You pull the pizza out and put it on the stovetop, shutting the door and turning to answer him. "I drank it last night." You're about to tell him you're sorry, even though you shouldn't, but you don't get the chance.

"You drank my fucking beer?"

You ought to tell him to calm down, that it's no big deal, but you can't help yourself. "Why not, I paid for it."

And he turns and walks out.

When you wake up the next morning, the pizza's still sitting there, cold and ruined, and Duane's still gone.

You shower, dress, and close up your suitcase, and an hour later, you're gone too.

You meet Doug at the airport and end up talking shop until you're on the plane. He tells you that you've got great instincts.

"I brought my red dress," you tell him.

"Don't wear it. Plain business suits. No nonsense."

You tell him you know men better than he does and mention Vogelman, and he looks at you and tells you that you got lucky, because these committees have lots of women on them and they can get pissy when a PYT shows up looking like they wished they looked twenty years ago.

"PYT?"

He looks at you and grins before emptying his tiny vodka bottle into his tomato juice. "Pretty young thing."

You laugh. "I should have known. Is that what I am?"

He looks at you serious. "You're a lot more than that. But yes, you've certainly got that going."

He gulps down his drink and you push at his arm in a playful way, having already downed your second whisky sour. "You're such a flirt!" *He's not the only one.*

He looks serious, though, and you know he means it. "You could be a great salesman."

You think to order a third drink but realize you've had enough, and you fold your arms and lean back, warm and content, basking in the compliment. And you know right there that you're going to sleep with him. Not tonight. Maybe not tomorrow night. But you like him, you like him a lot. You know he's got a wife, but she sounds as bad as Duane—bitchy and jealous and never giving him enough attention. So screw it, it's every man for himself. Or every woman for herself. Doug's wife certainly isn't worried about you. And neither is Grantham. So screw him too.

You pick up your cup and tilt it back into your mouth, sucking on an ice cube before giving him a sly look out the corner of your eye. "So, are we getting one room or two?"

The hotel is much nicer than the last one. "$140 a night," Doug tells you. "That's over 400 bucks apiece with tax."

You check in as Mr. and Mrs. Doug Smith, expecting the worst, but the man behind the counter doesn't bat an eyelash. This is the Marriott, prim and proper and corporate.

The room's got two king-sized beds, which is ok with you—everything in its time—and you take the bed near the window, further from the air conditioning vent, remembering how cold he likes it.

You unpack, go over a few more things for the first meeting tomorrow, and head out for dinner. He decides to save the rib place for another night, and you eat in the hotel dining room, still on the company dime, and you have a steak and so does he, and you're relieved to be out of St. Louis and that apartment and away from your cubicle.

You go to bed early, sleeping in sweats, and are up by five.

It's a long day, but the weather is perfect. The tail end of Indian summer, but they're much tougher than Vogelman and the folks in Iowa. The head honcho is a middle-aged black woman named Dawn, and you're glad you left that red dress back in the hotel room. Conservative business suit. Not threatening. Like Doug said.

You tell her about the discounts for bulk sales, but she's tough, wanting more. She questions how well your books will work with minority students and you tell her they work fine with all students, and she asks if you're in a position to judge, since you're white. And you tell her you're married to a black man, expecting that to warm things up, but it makes it worse.

"Another black man wasted on some lily white chick from god knows where," she mumbles under her breath just loud enough for you to hear.

You look at her. "You want him, you can have him." You start to collect your papers. "He's a bum."

She looks at you, and you're not sure how to read her. And Doug is holding his breath. But you're so pissed at Duane, you just let it rip. "You know, he used to tell me, 'When you've had black, you never go back.' Only now I'm pretty much ready to never go back to either."

Your emotions are raw and hanging out, and she puts her arm around you, and you didn't expect it. And she nods.

"Oh boy, you've got it bad, honey."

"I'm sorry," you say. You feel like a fool and you're ready to cry.

She takes her arm off you, and it's just the three of you, and she breaks the silence. "Don't worry honey, you'll get through it."

And you look at her and believe her, like she knows, and now it's like it's just the two of you, and for an instant, there's no one else in the world, and she puts her hands on her hips, defiant, triumphant, and reassuring, and she tells you, "Divorced twelve years. Two kids. Single mom."

You smile at her fighting back tears, and she grins. "Don't worry, sweetie, we'll buy your textbooks."

Later, back in the room, Doug can still hardly believe it.

"You were awesome."

He's sitting at the desk, but you're standing, arms folded, still wound up. "I wasn't selling," you tell him.

"The best salesmen never are. That's their genius." He looks right at you. "You were brilliant."

You shake your head and laugh a little. He's sweet. You know you could have him any time now, but you're all in knots. You could use something to relax but you don't want a drink.

He seems to sense it and next thing you know, he produces a little canister, popping the top open and pulling out a joint.

You look at him, incredulous but amused. "You brought that in your suitcase?"

"Why do you think I checked my bag?"

You shake your head, still smiling at him, unfolding your arms. "You *are* a bad boy."

You smoke one and then another, sitting next to him at the foot of your bed, in your slip, bare-legged and feeling great. It was exactly what you needed.

He passes the last of it back to you and you wrap your mouth tight around the roach, sucking it in deep, holding it, and blowing out.

Duane had a phrase for it, but you try to put it out of your mind. He always seemed to love tweaking you with the n-word. Then you put him out of your mind too.

You lean over and kiss Doug. It's slow and sultry, your mouths touching. And you feel his hands on you, your torso, working up your ribs but stopping short of your breasts, then caressing you and moving back up again. It's been a long time—seven and a half months—and this guy really knows what he's doing.

You kiss and touch for just long enough, then you lay back and tell him that you want him, and he crawls up on you, and you're ready to lift up your slip, but you put your hand on his chest. "Do you have protection?"

You can see from his face that he doesn't. And you don't either. You weren't exactly planning this when you were packing back in St. Louis, and, you can see, neither was he.

You sit up at the foot of the bed, and he does too, and you look at him, tender, a boy, a man, sweet and bad, someone who wants you more than anything, and you don't want to lose the moment. So you work his zipper free and go down. You can feel his delight, your face in his hands, stroking your hair. And you know you're in control, setting the tone, sweet and hot. Definitely hot. Wherever it goes.

You wake up in his arms, and you both smile, and he starts kissing you again, but you have more meetings, and you scramble to get dressed. You can see him watching you, standing in a thong at the mirror, but it'll have to wait.

The day seems to go on forever, avoiding eye contact, talking eighth grade science books and lab manuals, until it's almost five, and you're free.

You rush back, getting a box of condoms at a drugstore on the way, until you're finally back in your room. You plug your iPod in, putting on "You Can't Sit Down," by the Phil Upchurch Combo, and you take your clothes off slowly, until you're back down to that thong.

Then you undress him, slowly undoing his tie, unbuttoning his shirt, and taking off his belt. You turn off the air, thinking he might object, but he doesn't even seem to notice.

His chest is big and smooth with better definition that you'd expect from a textbook salesman. Pretty soon, the only thing between you and him is that thong, and you lay back, and he peels it off and takes you.

Afterward, you have the urge to tell him that you love him, but you don't. But the truth is, you haven't felt this good in a long, long time. Wanted. Loved. The air is still off, and you play with the sweat on his chest, telling him how you wanted to be a dancer, but you ended up working at Starbucks in Saginaw, which is where you met Duane. And he was cool and talented and handsome and wanted to play the blues. So you married him and moved to St. Louis.

And he starts touching you, and you're ready to go again.

By the time Friday rolls around, you don't want to leave.

"We can stay the extra night, leave Saturday. Even Sunday," he tells you, still in his boxers, putting on a shirt, getting ready for that last set of meetings.

"Oh come on! They're not stupid," you say, brushing your teeth in front of the bathroom mirror, just out of the shower, half-naked.

"I'll just tell them I'm sick and need the extra day." You see him in the mirror. He shrugs that bad boy shrug, naughty, sexy, and charming all at the same time. "Food poisoning. Happens all the time."

You spit, wipe your mouth, and talk to him through the mirror. "How come I didn't get it?"

"You had the lobster. I had the steak. Wasn't cooked enough."

"Raw meat. You're such a cave man."

You can see him staring at your breasts, and just like that, he wants you again.

And you put on "Soul Twist" by King Curtis, and you do a little dance for him, slow and sexy, in nothing but your thong, moving over him, easy, until he looks like he'll explode, and you laugh, straddle his knee and start kissing him.

"Did you used to be a stripper?" he asks, like a little boy.

"No!" you say, a little offended but a little flattered that he thinks you've got the body for it. And the moves.

You end up late for that last set of meetings, and Doug tells them that the cab broke down, but Dawn isn't buying it. "You watch out for that one," she tells you, and you're afraid your look gives you away, but she's turned to tell the head of the science department at Jackson High to make sure he orders enough books, and she doesn't see.

You get the extra sales, and when Doug reports back to the home office, telling them he's sick, they're happy to let you take the extra time. "Stay 'til Sunday if you need to," you hear Cathy say through Doug's cell phone, and you realize you've become a team, the stars of the Grantham sales force. So you take the weekend.

You stay in all day Saturday and make love. You haven't even texted Duane since Wednesday, and you don't care. He's carrying on with some bimbo somewhere anyway.

You break out the red dress on Saturday night, and Doug takes you to a fancy place on the Westside of town, and you want to go dancing after, but you come back again for a private session, and by the time you leave, you're ready.

Doug pushes five hundred bucks at you, and you wonder for a second what the extra cash is about, until he tells you, "Two more days, weekend rate. I'll put in for it when we get back," and you laugh.

"I guess I'm a bad girl too." And you feel the exhilaration and end up letting him take you in the airplane lavatory, like some crazy movie.

"Mile high club," he grins at you, and you're not even sure it's his first time.

"Guess I can die happy now," you say, nestled back in your seat.

And you get back to St. Louis, back to your place, and are surprised to see Duane there with two friends, sitting on the couch talking shop. They stop when they see you, but you're glad they're there, because it breaks the tension, and they're on their way out anyway.

You're exhausted and pull off your jeans as soon as they leave, and it feels a little funny to do that in front of Duane now, and the guilt hits you like a wave.

He notices and asks what's wrong, but you push it out of your mind. "Just tired. You won't believe how many meetings we had this week."

And you think for a second that he wants to, wants to touch you, and it turns out he does, but you push him off. "Sorry. I'm too tired," and he nods, and you fall off to sleep without even finishing to get undressed or wash up.

And back at work, you've made a big enough impression to get a private meeting with Eric, and he tells you and Doug that the old man wants to send you out to more of the bigger markets—Detroit, Pittsburgh, Cleveland, even Chicago. And that would mean every other week on the road, and you look at Doug, and Eric says, "I know you're both married, and it's asking a lot, but we'll make it up to you." He looks at you more than Doug, and you can tell that he thinks he's being persuasive, but you feel like laughing in his face. "You can say no," he says, and you sit there, eyebrows knitted, like you're thinking about it, and you tell him, "Let me talk to my husband." And the conversation ends with, "Of course. Take your time."

A minute later, in the stairwell, you jump up into Doug's arms, straddling his waist, giggling.

He flashes you a pleased look but eases you down with a whisper. "We have to be careful." But it's $1,000 a month. And all the sex you can muster. With pretty much no chance of getting caught. And you're having trouble containing yourself.

You never talk to Duane about any of it, telling Eric that it was a tough decision, but you're in. You finally get those bills cleared and get ready for your next trip. Detroit.

It scares you a little. It's only a hundred miles from home, so you're afraid you'll see somebody you know, even

though it's unlikely. And it's big and burned out and danger-
ous. And it all excites you a little. And before you know it,
you're there, staying at the Ford Center, giving another pitch.

The head of the district is black here too, but it's a man.
You find out ahead of time and dress a little sexier. You
make sure to mention about Duane. Just a hint of flirt to
soften him up, but this one's all business. Maybe you have to
be, in Detroit.

It's not going well, and by Monday afternoon, you think
maybe the trip will end up short. You and Doug go into his
office for another meeting, but he's not there. He calls. There
was a shooting at one of the high schools in South Detroit.
A couple of big athletes involved. And a teacher down. He
tells you to wait in his office; he'll be there within the hour.

Then Doug locks the door, and you can see what's coming next, but you can hardly believe it.

"No! No!" Heart racing, you look at him, "What if we
get caught?"

But he pushes you back, easy but firm, and you want to
resist, but you can't. And the next thing you know, he's got
you turned around, bent over the desk, pants down, and you
sink your teeth into one of your eighth grade science books
to stop from screaming.

And you can't believe how excited you are and how
good it feels and how long it's lasting. And when it's over,
you pull up your underwear and your pants, and you help

him tuck his shirt back in and ask him if you look ok. And he tells you, "Yes, beautiful," and you believe him.

And a minute later, the superintendant walks in, and you can tell he's rattled. You offer a sympathetic ear, and this warms things up, and you end up selling to over half the schools in the city, which is more than all of Cincinnati. And they'll need more replacement books down the line too.

There are only a couple of more meetings that you need to have and Doug spaces them out through the end of the week, and you spend the rest of the time with each other. You go shopping and buy yourself some new clothes. A cute sundress, even though it's starting to get colder out. And a pair of earrings, your first piece of jewelry since Duane bought you a necklace on your third anniversary.

You call your mother and your friend Stacy, who comes down to see you. She meets Doug, and you can tell that it makes him a little uncomfortable, but you tell her everything, and she says how cute he is but that she's worried about what you're getting yourself into. And when she uses that word, *stealing*, you wonder if you'll get caught and where it's all going.

But you hit a rhythm. A week in St. Louis, a week on the road. Sales pitches and sex in hotels. A controlled affair. And money coming in. Not a lot to most people, maybe, but it's a lot to you.

And, for the first time in your life, you really feel excited. Then, one night, in a hotel room in Pittsburgh, you tell him that you love him. And you're surprised when he does the same.

"Well, what are we going to do about it?" you ask.

And he tells you he doesn't know.

"That's not the answer I wanted."

"I've got two little girls."

And now the ball's back in your court, and you think about what it would be like to be a stepmom or even raise them.

And then your phone rings. You don't recognize the number, but it's St. Louis, and you answer.

"You bitch."

And just like that, you know it's over.

"I hope you both go to jail."

Your blood runs cold, but you say nothing.

"Yeah, I know about that too." Then the phone clicks dead.

Doug looks at you. "What's wrong?"

And you show him the number, and he's trying to figure out how his wife found out, and you scramble, getting dressed, putting on your underwear, like it matters now, like somehow that'll cancel it all out, like it was some big misunderstanding.

And you talk about the money. "She wouldn't tell Grantham," Doug says, more confident that he should be.

Then you wonder about Duane.

It's all going to hit the fan, you know. But you're surprisingly calm. It's a Thursday afternoon. You've got one more meeting, tomorrow. You wonder if you can reschedule to get it done today and maybe fly back tonight. Try to calm things. Damage control.

You pull up your pants, button up your blouse, and tuck it in. You're put back together, ready to go in another few minutes, looking yourself over in the mirror. It's a nice pantsuit, you think, navy blue, conservative. Hides those stripper's hips.

Looking over at Doug, you see him sitting there, still in his boxers, pale as a ghost. "Come on, get dressed." You reach for your cell phone. "I'm going to call, see if we can move the meeting to today." You look at your phone. It's almost three. "If we can meet in the next hour or two, we can fly back tonight."

He looks at you, like what's the point, and it sends a chill through you, because he knows her better than you do. Then the phone rings right there in your hand. It's Grantham. The old man, you think. Then you realize it's the company, not the person, but that hardly matters, and you answer.

"Hi Kerry. Bob Beck."

Beck, head of accounting. "What can I do for you?"

"We'd like to see you."

"Sure. We're in Pittsburgh right now—"

But he cuts you off. "I know. We've got some accounting irregularities that we need you and your partner to help straighten out."

"We have meetings—"

"They've been cancelled."

"Sure thing."

"Just you and Doug get on the plane. There's one leaving at five. And come straight here."

You have the urge to pack your suitcase and get on the next plane to Belize. Or at least back to Michigan. But you know it's ridiculous.

Doug is still sitting there, and you tell him to snap out of it, and he asks what's the point, and you sit down on the bed next to him, and he puts his arm around you, and you both take a deep breath.

Then you pack, check out, and head to the airport.

You look at him when he folds the receipt. Then, finally, in the cab, you ask him. "What are we going to say?"

And you see his look, and you know he's more worried about what he's going to say to his wife. And you can see that he still loves her. You think about those two little girls, and how did it come to this, with you, now the other woman.

Then you wonder aloud if she told Duane and how she figured it out. And it seems so strange that she'd go to the company, or even that they'd figure it out at the same time. Then you both realize: It was the people at Grantham that figured it out and called her.

They didn't tell her about the two of you; they probably don't even know. "I'm sure they just asked about the hotel rooms and she figured it out."

You look at him like he's an idiot, because you're sure they've figured *that* out too. Not just stealing, but doing it on their dime.

You fold your arms and lean back. Thinking about all those sales and how much money you've made them, and now you're the one in trouble, and you start to get mad.

You get up to go to the bathroom, and your butt goes in his face, and you can feel his eyes on your ass before you squeeze out into he aisle, and you can hardly believe it, and you want to yell at him, tell him to get it together.

When you get back, you talk again about what to tell them, but neither one of you has a clue.

"How about the truth," you say, and he nods.

"Yeah. I'll tell them it was all my idea. You didn't know anything about it." He looks at you, resigned. "It's pretty much true, anyway."

Then you think about those girls again. "No, we'll tell them that it was both of us. We did it together."

"There's no reason—"

"They already know," you say, cutting him off.

He thinks for a second.

"So there's no point," you add, and the issue seems decided.

You cross your legs and fold your arms, closing your eyes, wanting it all to go away, trying not even to think about Duane, trying to sleep but unable to even come close, your mind racing a million miles and hour. *I'm going to go to jail,* you think.

You wonder what his wife is really like. Then you wonder about Duane. You can't really blame him for having an affair.

The plane starts to descend for landing, and a wave of terror hits you. *Going in to face the music.* And you panic. You can see it in Doug too.

You're quiet all the way to the office. It's almost 6:30 by the time you arrive. Walking back in with your suitcases in tow, it feels very different than the last time. Going in to meet your executioner. Bob Beck. At least you'll be together.

But when you get up to the office, it isn't just Beck. The old man is there too. His secretary gives you the stink eye, even though she barely makes any eye contact at all. And you think it's going to be the four of you in a room. But it's not.

"You take the conference room," the old man says to Beck.

And you think it's going to be you and the old man in his office, but you've got it that wrong too: Beck points you to the conference room, and it's Doug and Grantham in the office. *No feminine wiles to peddle here,* you think.

You walk into the conference room, and there's already someone there, another man in a suit, someone you don't recognize.

"This is Mr. Morgan from legal," Beck tells you. "You don't mind if he sits in," he says more than asks. Then he tells you to have a seat before you even answer.

This is going to be bad.

"Why don't you tell us what's going on," Beck starts.

You want to ask for an attorney of your own, but you can't afford one, and there doesn't seem to be any point. You don't know what to say, so you sit there with your mouth hanging open until Beck fills the silence again.

"Look Ms. Bergin, we paid for thousands of dollars worth of hotel rooms that you never used. Do you have an explanation?"

He's got you on the ropes. You want to cry, but you know these types. They'd just view it as another ploy, so you fight it off, looking down, shaking your head.

"I didn't catch that," the lawyer says.

You lift your head. "No."

"No what?"

"No, I don't have an explanation."

Beck leans over to the lawyer next to him and whispers in his ear. It's too low for you to hear, and then the lawyer writes something on his legal pad and shows it to Beck, who nods. For a second, you feel like *you're* back in high school. Except this is a whole lot worse.

Beck takes the lead again. "You're in a whole lot of trouble Ms. Bergin."

"Kerry," you tell him, not wanting to correct the 'Ms.,' but not wanting to hear it again either.

There's another long silence before Beck continues. "Look, we know it was all Doug's idea." He looks right at you. "There's no need for you take the blame." He leans in to you from across that long conference room table. "I don't think you'd do very well in jail. And we do intend to prosecute."

You look up at him, shocked. *They want to fry Doug for this.* And those two little girls won't leave your mind.

"You've got it all wrong," you tell him, suddenly confident and brazen. "Doug doesn't know anything about this. It was all me. I wasn't making enough." And you look at him right in the eye. "So I stole the money. It was me. I'm the one you want."

He looks shocked, and even the lawyer raises his eyebrows and writes on his pad.

"Is that your position?" Beck asks, like he can hardly believe it.

"Yes."

And you feel good for the first time all day.

"So you planned the whole thing out."

"Yeah. It was me."

"Bullshit."

You keep your stoneface on, and he seems to get that you're not going to budge, although you know he doesn't buy it. But you don't care. It's the right thing, you tell yourself.

The two men leave you alone for what seems like forever, until Beck comes back with Grantham, Doug, Morgan, and another man in tow.

The men sit, and for a second it feels like a board meeting. Or at least what you imagine one to be like.

Then Grantham gestures to the man you don't know and then to Morgan. "You two can go."

Morgan folds up his pad in a leather case, pops his expensive-looking ballpoint, slipping it inside, gets up, and heads for the door. But the other man doesn't move so fast.

"That's against council's recommendation," he tells Grantham.

Grantham waves him off, annoyed. "Yeah, yeah. Save all the legal bull. No lawyers."

The man raises his eyebrows in disapproval and gets up, taking his pad and pen—a plain yellow legal pad and what looks like a Bic ballpoint—with him.

"You're the boss." He forces a smile at Grantham, and you can see he's been around for a long time, graying at the temples, but the relationship is not warm.

A moment later, it's just the four of you. Beck looks uncertain and starts to rise but Grantham motions for him to sit, even though you figure he probably doesn't need him at this point.

And here it comes.

"You know, I trusted you two. And what did you do? You stole. You screwed me. I consider this company like my family. We sell textbooks, so kids can learn, and you two turned it into your personal slush fund."

Suddenly, you're not so sure he knows about the affair. And you keep listening, nodding in silence, hoping for the best.

"We split you up. That was the lawyers' idea. We wanted to hear what kind of bull you'd come up with. Then we'd pull it apart and corner you and watch you point the finger at each other. The lawyers said that's what would happen at any rate. Then we'd press charges, turn you over to the courts."

He looks over at Doug. Then right at you. "But that's not what happened." He pauses, still surprised himself. "You each took the blame for the other."

You wait to see where this is going.

"At least you have loyalty to someone if not me."

He waves his hand, looking away from you both in disgust, grasping the opportunity to be done with the whole matter. "Just get out of here. You're both fired. I don't want to see either one of you ever again. You'll make arrangements with Bob to pay the money back. And if you don't, we're coming after you." He turns around and looks straight at you, still sitting there. "Now get out of here! I don't want to see either of you again."

And just like that, it's over. Beck tells you both you'll get an agreement in the mail that says you'll pay back what you took, and that if you don't, Grantham will press charges. There's also a breech of confidentiality clause, a kind of gag order that says that you can never discuss any of this. And a non-compete clause that says you can never work for any of Grantham's competitors or anywhere in the textbook business again. And the final plume: That you agree not to talk with or see each other ever again.

Doug tells you afterward that the last part is unenforceable, but regardless, you know you'll never see him again. He seems to know too.

He touches your cheek. "Thanks for sticking up for me."

"You too."

And you hug him before racing off, not wanting to cry in front of him.

It starts raining. It's been threatening all afternoon, and now that evening has arrived, so has the rain. So you walk home and think about Duane and what you're going to do.

The apartment is empty when you get there. But there's music spread out over the bed. And you see that it's his writing, something he's been working on, an original composition. He always said he'd write a piece of music for you, but you'd forgotten about it.

Then you realize, that's where he's been when he's disappeared, coming back late or even staying out all night. He's been holed up, working on the piece, *Sonata for Kerry Blue.*

And you realize how much you love him and what you're about to lose, and suddenly you have to find him. You call, but his phone rings right there in the apartment, where he left it. Yes, you have to find him, tell him everything, hope he forgives you, hope he takes you back.

You shower and put on the best dress you've got, a blue satin number that's elegant and sleek, and you head out, barely able to contain your emotions. *Kerry Blue.*

You go to all the clubs and haunts that you know, there amongst the warehouses and over on the other side of 7th Street and then back across again, all the way to the river. It's raining hard now, and you start to cry, alone in the wet, your dress ruined, your love seemingly lost. And you run, breaking your heel, then pulling both shoes off and running in your stocking feet in the pouring rain.

The tears are flowing and the rain washes over you, and you hear it, faintly at first, then louder as you make your way towards it. A sound. Music. A tenor saxophone. And you follow it, right to your building, until you can see it, pinned up high against the night sky. A saxophone, and a man playing it. Standing on the fire escape of the top floor. Your building. Your apartment. Your husband. Duane, blowing through. The most beautiful sound you've ever heard. The Sonata for Kerry Blue.

You come in, quiet, stepping through until you're at the open window, watching him play through the rain. You go to your knees and sit back on your heels, dripping and raw, until he finishes and steps inside, having drawn you in.

And you hug him, crying, and he hugs you back, and you start to tell him, but he stops you with a touch of his finger to your lips, because he already knows.

And you fall asleep in his arms, where you belong, listening to the rain, hearing his song, *your* song, and understanding it all for the first time.

To see our other great titles,
visit us at:

www.ingramcontent.com/pod-product-compliance
Lightning Source LLC
Chambersburg PA
CBHW031900170626
46807CB00004B/1820